The Junior Novelization

Special thanks to Diane Reichenberger, Cindy Ledermann, Ann McNeill, Kim Culmone, Emily Kelly, Sharon Woloszyk, Carla Alford, Rita Lichtwardt, Kathy Berry, Rob Hudnut, David Wiebe, Shelley Dvi-Vardhana, Gabrielle Miles, Technicolor, and Walter P. Martishius

Published in the United States by Random House Children's Books, a division of Random House, Inc., 1745 Broadway, New York, NY 10019, and in Canada by Random House of Canada Limited, Toronto. Random House and the colophon are registered trademarks of Random House, Inc.
ISBN: 978-0-307-98110-3
randomhouse.com/kids
Printed in the United States of America
10 9 8 7 6 5 4 3 2 1   First Edition

The Junior Novelization

Adapted by Molly McGuire Woods
Based on the screenplay by Alison Taylor
Illustrated by Ulkutay Design Group

Random House 🏠 New York

I dance to my own beat

Ballet keeps me on my toes

believe in dance

shining star

dancer at heart

in the spotlight

Dancer at heart

cent

e here I come

in the spotlight

believe in dance

Believe

shining star

dance and twirl like a Barbie girl

pointe your toes

Tu Tu

dancer at heart

believe

dream it. dance it.

shining star

Love

Barbie

believe in dance

ballet is the best

shining star

e to Dance

love to dance...

love to dream

of a dancer

In the Spotlight

lieve in dance

dancer at heart

center stage here I come

keeps me on my toes

shining star

Barbie

I dance

ter stage here I come

to my own beat

in the spotlight

pointe your toes

Love to Dance

love to dance...

dancer at

Barbie

I dance to my own be

Ballet keeps me on my toe

believe in dance

shining star

ancer at heart

dancer at heart

in the spotli

e here I come

in the spotlight

believe in dance

cent

Believe

shining star

dance and twirl like a Barbie girl

pointe your toes

Tu Tu

dancer at heart

believe

dream it. dance it.

shining star

Love

Barbie

believe in dance

ballet is the best

shining sta

Chapter 1

"Dakotah—arms! Casey—where are you looking? Gabrielle—smile!"

Kristyn Faraday stood in the wings of the stage in her black leotard, pink tights, and practice tutu. She watched her fellow dancers move as Madame Natasha, the lead instructor of her ballet academy, coached them through another rehearsal. *I hope Madame isn't this hard on me when it's my turn,* she worried.

Not that it would surprise her. To Kristyn, Madame's critiques were nothing new. Her instructor had been this strict for as long as Kristyn could remember. Madame Natasha believed there was only one way to do things in the world of ballet: her way. Practice and precision were everything. Madame even *looked* disciplined, with her silver hair pulled back into a tight bun on top of her head. She marched back and forth on long, lean dancer's legs as she evaluated every student's movement.

"And one and two and three and four . . . ," Kristyn whispered along as Madame Natasha counted to the rhythm of the classical music.

"Head up, Casey—watch the audience, not your feet! Now, on the beat . . . perrrrfect!" Madama Natasha purred.

Behind the curtain, Kristyn shared a look with her best friend, Hailey. They had watched this routine so many times, they knew what Madame Natasha was going to say before she did!

"Head direction, girls!" they whispered. "Stay together! Clean fifth! Tight angles, girls. Be precise!" The friends dissolved into giggles.

Just then, Dillon Matthews joined them. Dillon was the male lead dancer in the academy's performance of *Swan Lake*. He shook his blond hair out of his eyes and smiled at Kristyn.

Kristyn beamed. Was it just her or did Dillon

get better-looking every time she saw him? It didn't hurt that his dancing was some of the best she had ever seen.

But Hailey looked at Dillon's costume and frowned. She shoved a hand into a pocket of the apron she always wore and plucked out a pincushion and a pair of glasses. She held Dillon's arm down and set to work adjusting a shoulder on his jacket.

Kristyn smiled at her best friend's look of concentration. *Such a perfectionist!*

Hailey wasn't a dancer like Kristyn and Dillon were. Her passion was costume design. She wanted to have her own costume shop one day. But for now, helping Madame Katerina with the ballet company's wardrobe was like a dream come true. Hailey got to practice her sewing techniques, and Madame Katerina even let her come up with some of her own designs.

"And one and two and three and four . . ."

Kristyn danced pirouettes around Dillon and Hailey to the sound of Madame Natasha's counting onstage. "I can't believe I remember every single move of this dance!" she exclaimed.

Dillon chuckled. "It's drilled into my brain, too. You did it like six years in a row or something, right?" he asked Kristyn.

"Seven," Hailey corrected him, wrestling with his costume.

Dillon wriggled away from Hailey and danced a couple of the familiar steps himself.

"Dillon!" Hailey scolded. "Hold still!"

He stopped dancing and grinned.

Kristyn chuckled as Hailey rolled her eyes and tried to look serious. It was hard to be mad at someone as funny as Dillon.

Hailey took off his costume jacket and hung it on a nearby rack. "You are hereby ordered to stop growing," she commanded in her sternest voice, placing her sewing glasses carefully back in her apron pocket. "These sleeves fit you just last week."

The three friends cracked up.

Suddenly, Kristyn heard a sharp *"Shhh!"*

She glanced over her shoulder to see Tara Pennington, the prima ballerina in the company, edging her way toward Kristyn, Hailey, and Dillon.

"Shhh!" Tara scolded again.

"Sorry," Kristyn mumbled. Why did Tara always have to be so bossy?

Tara eased in front of them to get a better look at the rehearsal.

Not that she needs it, Kristyn thought. With three solos, Tara was the principal, or lead, female dancer in the company. Madame Natasha always saved the best dances for her. And there was no doubt about it: Tara was super talented. But it did make Kristyn jealous sometimes. Tara's snotty attitude didn't help.

Tara waved Dillon over to her. "Dillon, we're almost up," she announced.

"Since when are you the shush-monster?" Dillon asked. He gave Kristyn a wink.

Tara started to scowl but then thought better of it. She flashed a flirty smile at Dillon and leaned on his shoulder. "I'm sorry, guys," she whined dramatically. "I don't want to be a downer, but I have three solos to think about.

So can we have some focus, please?"

Kristyn could feel herself getting angry. Leave it to Tara to rub it in.

At that moment, the stage manager rushed toward them. She whisked Dillon and Tara away so that they could prepare to go on next.

Kristyn sighed heavily. "She's got three solos?" she said, more to herself than to anyone else. Kristyn knew her dancing was just as strong as Tara's, even if it was a little different. Tara was a classic ballerina. She danced with precision—exactly the way Madame Natasha instructed them. But Kristyn liked to add her own flavor to her dances. She couldn't help herself. Whenever the music started, it was like her body completely took over. She got lost in her performances, sometimes not following the choreography. That was why Tara—not Kristyn—would always be Madame Natasha's favorite.

Kristyn forced herself to focus once again on the rehearsal. Even though her part was toward the end, it was important to pay attention to the rhythm of the entire show.

Onstage, a group of younger dancers was rehearsing a complicated number. One of the dancers, Hannah, became dizzy from spinning and lost her balance. She crashed into the girl next to her, threatening to cause a chain reaction. Kristyn held her breath. Madame Natasha would not be pleased if they had to start the number again. But the dancers kept their cool and recovered. Kristyn sighed with relief as the music ended. *That was a close one.*

"It's almost there, girls," Madame Natasha said with a frown. "But continue to practice downstairs. Do it twenty or thirty more times." Madame Natasha strode toward the girl who had stumbled during the number. "You need to focus on every single step, Holly," she said, pinching the girl's cheek.

"It's Hannah," the girl whispered. She rubbed her cheek, which was now as pink as her tights.

"That's right, my dear," Madame Natasha said distractedly, looking over Hannah's shoulder. "Every move must be precise, exact, controlled.

You will be perfect." Hannah's lip quivered.

Kristyn winced along with the other dancers. *Poor Hannah*. No one liked to be singled out by their demanding instructor. Kristyn made a mental note to help Hannah with that section of the dance later.

Madame Natasha clapped her hands. "Now," she announced brightly. "Who's next?"

Chapter 2

"Last rehearsal before the show, Dillon. Let's make magic!" Tara sang as she grabbed Dillon's hand and pulled him toward the stage.

Kristyn took a breath and tried to calm the butterflies that were fluttering in her stomach. Tonight was the night! The dancers from Madame Natasha's company would be performing a showcase of some of their best numbers in front of talent scouts from an international ballet company. These scouts had discovered some of the most famous ballerinas in the world. If they liked what they saw tonight, they might consider casting some of the dancers in their company. Maybe they would even pick her! Kristyn pictured herself traveling the world, dancing night after night in beautiful theaters, audiences throwing roses at her feet as she performed. It would be amazing!

Just then, the music to *Swan Lake* swelled, snapping Kristyn back to reality. *Don't get ahead of yourself,* she thought as Tara and Dillon swept gracefully past her and took their positions onstage.

Suddenly, Hailey bounced up behind Kristyn. She put a reassuring hand on Kristyn's shoulder.

"She's soooo high-maintenance," Hailey said, eyeing Tara dancing onstage.

"And soooo good," Kristyn said, lost in the magic of the dance.

Dillon and Tara moved in sync in a pas de deux, or dance for two, in the second act of *Swan Lake.* Dillon was dancing the part of Siegfried, the prince, and Tara was dancing the part of Princess Odette. In the ballet, Odette is under an evil sorcerer's spell. During the day, she is trapped on the lake as a swan, and only when the sun sets can she return to her human form. Unless Prince Siegfried pledges his undying love to her, Odette will be trapped forever as a swan.

Kristyn thought it was a beautiful love story.

Kristyn couldn't take her eyes off Tara and Dillon. The stage lights played across their faces as they swayed in perfect time to the music. Kristyn heaved a sigh. *Just once,* she thought, *I'd like the chance.*

As Tara and Dillon moved around the stage, Kristyn allowed her eyes to wander out into the audience. She noticed Tara's father sitting in the front row, watching his daughter's every move. He was dressed in a slick suit and wore a fat gold watch. Kristyn knew that Mr. Pennington came to every rehearsal. He always seemed to have something to say about Tara's performances. Kristyn wondered if that ever made Tara nervous. It sure seemed like a lot of pressure.

Mr. Pennington watched Tara dance with precision. He counted the beat with his thick fingers, practically dancing in his seat, nodding when Tara leaped sideways three times in a perfect pas de chat.

Kristyn ventured a glance at Madame Natasha. She looked pleased, nodding at each of Tara's turns. There was no denying it: Tara's dancing was just plain beautiful.

"She's perfect," Kristyn said to Hailey, letting out a breath. "I wish I could dance like she does. Just for one day."

As the music died down, Dillon and Tara slowed to a stop. They took a deep bow and then breezed offstage into the wings. The rest of the company broke into applause.

"Thank you, thank you," Tara said graciously, breathing heavily. Someone handed her a towel, and she dried off dramatically.

"You guys were amazing," Kristyn said. She meant it, even if she was feeling a tad envious.

"Of course we weren't going all out," Tara scoffed, smiling tightly. "Saving something for the show tonight." She turned toward her partner. "That's why those positions were so sloppy, right, Dillon?"

Dillon arched an eyebrow in surprise. "Sloppy?"

Kristyn gave him a warm smile. "You looked perfect to me, Dillon," she said.

Tara pulled a face. "Really?" she said. "We've got more work to do than I thought." She shot Dillon a look.

On the stage, Madame Natasha clapped her hands again to get everyone's attention. "Who's next?" she called, scanning her clipboard. "Let's have the milkmaid number! Bring in the cow!"

In the wings, Kristyn straightened her shoulders. *My time to shine,* she thought. She adjusted her tutu and did some work on the ballet barre backstage to loosen up.

Hailey gave her a high five. "Bucket?" she asked.

"Check," Kristyn replied, picking up her prop.

The music rose, giving Kristyn her cue. *Let's do this,* she said to herself.

"Just get out there and dance like nobody's watching!" Hailey said.

Tara gave a mean chuckle. "Because nobody will be watching . . . except the cow!"

Dillon frowned. "A simple 'break a leg' would have sufficed," he grumbled.

Leave it to Tara to try and ruin my focus. Sure,

the milkmaid role wasn't the most important, but every piece in a showcase served a purpose. Kristyn loved dancing so much it almost didn't matter what role she was cast in . . . almost. Kristyn took a deep, cleansing breath. She raised her arms in port de bras and pranced onstage.

Chapter 3

Kristyn took her place onstage next to a papier-mâché cow. She closed her eyes and took in her favorite part of any performance—the moment before it all began. For Kristyn, there was no better feeling than being onstage: the dust under her toe shoes, the warm stage lights on her face, the hush of the crowd as they waited for the next number. It was like the whole world was holding its breath for her.

The music began. Kristyn circled her arms and raised herself en pointe. As she moved through her routine, out of the corner of her eye, she could see Madame Natasha nodding in approval. As always, she could feel Hailey's support from the wings.

Kristyn loved how beautiful and strong

dancing made her feel—like she could do anything. She felt her chest swell with the melody and all of the sudden she had an inspiration. Using her milk bucket as a step, she raised herself high in the air. She let her sharp, classical movements become loose and expressive. She danced from the heart and felt herself lifted above the music as she spun.

In the wings, Hailey winced as she watched Kristyn improvise. "Oh, no!" she gasped.

Tara turned to Hailey. "That isn't the choreography," she said with a scowl. "What's she doing?"

"Something awesome that's going to get her in a whole sack of trouble!" Dillon responded with a grin.

Hailey waved her hand, brushing everyone away. "Shhh!" she hushed. "A little focus, please?"

Kristyn startled at the sound of Madame Natasha's booming voice.

"Stop! Stop the music! Stop *everything*!" the instructor hollered.

Kristyn stumbled, struggled to regain her balance, and landed on the side of her foot. *Riiiip.*

She looked down and gasped. "Argh," she groaned as she noticed her torn toe shoe. Kristyn lost her footing and crumbled to the floor, taking the cow prop down with her. Hailey cringed.

"This is cutting into my rehearsal time," Tara said impatiently, glancing at the clock.

"Shush!" Hailey scolded her.

"What are you, a librarian?" Tara snapped.

"Shush!" Dillon echoed, glaring at his partner. He raced onstage to Kristyn's side.

An angry Madame Natasha stormed across the stage, her low heels hitting each step hard. "Miss Faraday," she barked. "That is not the choreography we rehearsed," Madame Natasha barked.

Kristyn looked into the furious face of her instructor. "I know," she admitted sheepishly. "Got a little carried away there."

Madame Natasha crossed her arms and tapped her foot. "Miss Faraday. I assume you want to impress the international ballet scouts who will be here tonight?"

Kristyn hung her head. "Uh . . . yes, Madame."

"If that's the case," her instructor continued, "then I strongly suggest you follow the choreography and technique I have given you. I've seen other girls attempt to dance their own ideas, and I promise you that story does not end well."

Kristyn sighed. The truth was she hadn't intended to veer so far off course during her performance. "I don't mean to, Madame," she said earnestly. "I just get caught up in the music and the flow, and my feet just . . . do their own thing."

Madame Natasha wagged a long finger at

Kristyn. "You can do your 'own thing' if you want, Miss Faraday, but keep this up and after tonight you will have to do it somewhere else."

Kristyn bit her bottom lip. "Yes, Madame," she whispered. In her head, Kristyn knew that Madame Natasha only wanted what was best for her, but in her heart, she couldn't help but wonder if maybe there was another way. In any case, she knew she'd have to try harder if tonight's showcase was to be a success.

"Now, please get yourself some new shoes," Madame said, eyeing Kristyn's foot. "Take five, everyone!" she shouted, and stomped away.

Dillon helped Kristyn to her feet. "Are you okay?" he asked.

Kristyn brushed some dust from her knee. "Thanks. I'm fine," she replied, trying to conceal the smile that was creeping across her face. Even though she was in trouble, Kristyn couldn't hide the high she felt after dancing. What she had told Madame Natasha was the truth: she had never meant to change the routines. But her body had just taken over. Plus, while it may have cost her some harsh words from Madame, it also meant that Dillon was standing right next to her, helping her to her feet. *Not bad for a day's work.*

"Dillon!" Tara shouted angrily, marching toward them.

"Come on, Kristyn," Hailey said, joining them. "Let's get you some new shoes."

Meanwhile, out in the audience, Mr. Pennington gathered his things and shoved them into his knapsack. He stormed toward Madame Natasha.

"Tara can do it," he said. Mr. Pennington unzipped his backpack and rummaged around. He pulled out a foil pouch and popped some of its contents into his mouth.

Madame Natasha looked up from her clipboard. "I'm sorry, what?"

"Tara can do that solo for the Faraday girl," Mr. Pennington said, his mouth full. "Where are my manners?" he continued. He offered Madame the packet. "Turkey jerky? All protein."

Madame scorched him with a look of disgust. "I'll set the lineup *after* rehearsal, as I please," she replied sternly. "No one is in or out until I say so."

Mr. Pennington studied her seriously. "This is Tara's big night, so I don't want anything to spoil it. Are we on the same page?" He waved two fingers back and forth, pointing from his eyes to Madame's.

Madame gave a small nod. "The international ballet scouts will see plenty of Tara," she assured him.

But Mr. Pennington was unsatisfied. "What *else* will they see?" he cried, waving his arms. "Falling cows? Check. An octopus in a milkmaid costume? Double check. Is that the kind of program—"

Madame held up her hand and fixed an icy stare on Mr. Pennington. "My program is *not* in question here, Mr. Pennington. Are we clear?"

Mr. Pennington met her gaze. "Crystal,"

he replied. Then he looked around and pulled his jacket closed. "Who's blasting the AC? It's freezing."

Madame Natasha raised her chin. "The temperature is absolutely perrrrrrfect!" she said. Then she spun on her heel and walked away.

Chapter 4

Kristyn and Hailey entered the costume room behind the theater. Next to being onstage, this was Kristyn's favorite place. It was so warm and cozy, with rack after rack of costumes and bolts of brightly colored tulle, silk, and satin. Kristyn loved the feeling it gave her of being a part of something big. Surrounded by all of the costumes from some of the greatest ballet productions in the world, Kristyn felt special and lucky. Plus, this was Hailey's spot. Just as Hailey supported Kristyn onstage, Kristyn loved to be a part of Hailey's world.

The girls moved past racks of costumes and props of all kinds. Finally, Kristyn sank into an overstuffed chair and sighed. She began untying her toe shoes.

"Madame Katerina!" Hailey called as she disappeared down a costume aisle.

A walking mass of sparkling tutus bumbled around the corner.

Kristyn recognized Madame Katerina, the head costume designer, instantly. She grinned. Kristyn didn't think she had ever seen Madame when she wasn't covered in sequins, glitter, and tulle.

As Madame Katerina moved through the space, she deposited tutus on mannequins and hangers until her pile diminished enough to reveal her warm eyes behind it. She looked at Kristyn kindly. "I saw the whole thing," she said, taking a tutu off her arm and laying it on a worktable littered with crystals and silver thread. "Beautiful dancing. Like a butterfly."

Kristyn frowned. "Madame Natasha didn't think so. I got too caught up in the flow. Again."

From deep within one of the costume rows, Kristyn heard Hailey's voice, muffled by fabric. "Madame, do we have even one extra pair of size fives left?" she asked, looking for a spare pair for Kristyn but unable to find anything.

"Shoes?" Madame Katerina replied. "There should be some extras over by the *Giselle* costumes."

"It will take more than new shoes for me to make Madame Natasha happy tonight." Kristyn pouted. "I was far from 'perrrrfect.'"

Madame Katerina clucked her tongue. "Nonsense, my dear."

Kristyn gave her a grateful smile and ambled in the direction of Hailey's voice. She absentmindedly picked up a tiara on a worktable and ran her fingers along the jewels and feathers.

"When I'm dancing, I know the moves, of course, but suddenly I think of a thousand new ways to do them. Then those new moves just . . . start moving!" She placed the tiara back on the table and continued down the aisle. She joined Hailey in front of a stunning blue gown hanging on a dress dummy.

"Ohhh, Giselle," Kristyn said, sidetracked. She touched the rich fabric of the dress.

Hailey chuckled. She pulled out colorful

boxes of shoes, looking for the right pair for Kristyn. "She's been this way forever, Madame. She knows every role and every step, but when it's time to perform, she just . . . There are no size fives here."

Kristyn took the gown off the mannequin and held it to her chest. She danced an effortless arabesque. "I would give anything to dance Giselle," she said with a sigh.

Giselle was probably her favorite ballet. The story was about a common peasant, Giselle, who fell in love with a prince in disguise, only to die of a broken heart when she learned his true identity. *It doesn't get more romantic than that,* Kristyn thought.

Madame Katerina joined them. "Careful," she said, eyeing the gown Kristyn held. "We're not quite done with that one yet." She turned to Hailey. "Try over in *Swan Lake* storage."

Lost in her thoughts, Kristyn returned the dress to the wrong mannequin and trailed behind Hailey. "Tara's so lucky," she mused, noticing Dillon's costume jacket on a nearby mannequin.

"Madame will never trust me with a lead role."
She spotted her own plain milkmaid costume
on another dress dummy. She picked it up and
moved in front of a mirror.

"But your milkmaid dance is a delight!"
Madame Katerina exclaimed.

Kristyn frowned. "Oh, I wish I could dance
Giselle, or just once be Odette, queen of
the swans." She replaced her costume and
meandered into the next aisle, where Hailey
had found another stack of shoe boxes to sift
through.

"Size seven, size eight . . . ," Hailey mumbled.
"Still no fives."

Kristyn pulled an exquisite purple tutu off a
nearby hanger and held it in front of herself in
the mirror.

Madame Katerina appeared behind her in the
mirror's reflection. She placed a sympathetic
hand on Kristyn's shoulder. "I wanted that, too,"
she whispered. "But Natasha got all the dancing
talent in our family."

Kristyn had forgotten that Madame Katerina

and Madame Natasha were sisters. They certainly didn't act alike! She'd never heard Madame Katerina talk about being onstage herself. It made her wonder if Hailey ever thought about dancing instead of working behind the scenes.

"Size five!" Hailey announced triumphantly. "Nope. It's a seven," she said, discarding another box.

Kristyn smiled at her friend. Hailey seemed pretty at home in the costume shop. Kristyn turned down the next aisle. "Ahhh!" she cried, suddenly stopping in her tracks.

An imposing white costume stood on a mannequin before her. Something about it gave Kristyn the chills. Covered in icy crystals and silver embroidery, it was the most beautiful— and threatening—costume Kristyn had ever seen. She shuddered. *Who would wear such a scary costume?*

Madame Katerina appeared. "Our holiday production this year," she remarked, adjusting something at the back of the wintry masterpiece. *"The Snow Queen."*

Kristyn nodded warily, thinking about the story of the evil Snow Queen and how she tried to control everyone around her. *Sounds a little like someone else I know*, Kristyn thought, picturing Madame Natasha wearing the Snow Queen costume. "Does Tara wear this, too?" she asked, feeling a slight shiver.

Madame Katerina shook her head. "Not this one."

"Doesn't matter," Kristyn said bitterly. "I'm sure I'll be wearing antlers and pulling a sleigh."

Just then, Hailey came flying around the corner. "Plenty of shoes, Madame," she announced, brushing her hair out of her face. "But no fives. And all the stores are closed."

Madame Katerina put her finger to her chin and thought. "Wait," she said, disappearing behind a nearby curtain. "I might have something here."

Kristyn and Hailey exchanged a puzzled look.

A few minutes later, Madame Katerina returned, carrying an antique-looking box. She handed it gently to Kristyn.

Kristyn examined the box. She certainly had never bought shoes that came in such lovely packaging before. She carefully lifted the lid to reveal a pair of bright pink satin toe shoes. "Oh!" she gasped. "They're beautiful!"

Hailey lifted the shoes out of the box. "Right size, wrong color," she declared.

"No way!" Kristyn countered. "Pink is always in style."

"They're for you, my dear," Madame Katerina stated.

Kristyn smiled gratefully. "Thank you," she whispered, not taking her eyes off the hot-pink shoes. She walked to a nearby bench and quickly slipped one shoe on. It fit perfectly.

"You know, I bet I can bleach them to match your costume," Hailey offered, sitting on the bench next to Kristyn.

Kristyn slipped on the other shoe and expertly tied both around her ankles. "Wow!" she exhaled. "These are some shoes!"

Hailey took Kristyn's hand to help her stand en pointe. "Madame," Hailey called over her shoulder. "You had these all along?"

But Madame was nowhere to be seen.

Strange, thought Kristyn. *She was here just a moment ago.*

Suddenly, a swirl of glittery magic spun around Kristyn and Hailey. Kristyn felt dizzy. What was happening?

Then everything went black.

Chapter 5

"Whoa," Hailey said, steadying herself.

Kristyn rubbed her eyes and took in her surroundings. The girls stood on a path shaded by tall trees. They could see houses in the distance.

"Hailey. Where are we, and what am I wearing?" Kristyn asked, looking down at the rich blue dress she suddenly had on.

"I have no idea, and you are wearing Tara's Giselle dress," Hailey replied matter-of-factly.

"Tara's dress?" Kristyn cried. Things were not making sense. Just a moment ago they'd been in the cozy comfort of the costume shop, and now here they were in some sort of forest! And she was wearing Tara's magnificent blue Giselle costume. She ran her hand along the lush tulle of the dress. "Where did it come from?"

"Madame Katerina did the bodice and I did the skirt, but the fabric is from India, so technically—"

"No," Kristyn interrupted Hailey. "I mean how did I get into this dress?"

"Uh," Hailey said, eyeing Kristyn's head. "I guess the same way your hair turned strawberry blond."

Kristyn's hands flew to her head. "What?" she cried.

Hailey searched her apron pocket and pulled out a mirror. She held it out for Kristyn to take a look.

Kristyn gazed at her reflection. Yup. Strawberry blond. What was going on?

Just then, the friends heard music playing in the background.

"Wait!" Hailey exclaimed. "I know that music."

Kristyn nodded. She recognized it, too. It was a piece from *Giselle*, played during the scene when the villagers gather to crown Giselle the

Queen of the Harvest. But why was it playing here, now, on this forest path . . . with three houses in the distance? "These houses," she started. "It's like we're in *Giselle*."

Hailey stared at her, wide-eyed. "But how could we be in *Giselle?*"

Kristyn peered into the distance. "I don't know," she remarked. "But if we are, the maidens are about to appear. Here they come!" She pointed across the clearing.

The girls dashed to the side of one of the houses and waited as dancers entered from stage right and filled the square. They began to move.

"Look," Kristyn said. "The peasants are about to crown Giselle as Queen of the Harvest." She couldn't believe her eyes.

Just then, a man appeared onstage. "And there's Albrecht, the prince," Kristyn explained, pointing at a very handsome and regal-looking young man dressed as a peasant.

Hailey nodded. She knew this story almost as well as Kristyn did. She scowled at Albrecht.

"Jerk," she whispered under her breath. "Engaged to another girl and still trying to date Giselle. Where's the nice guy, Hilarious or whatever?"

"Hilarion," Kristyn corrected her friend, remembering the sweet farmer from the ballet who also loved Giselle. "He's hiding, I guess."

"Of course he is," Hailey replied sarcastically. "And we're in a ballet and pigs are about to fly and—"

"No. No flying pigs," Kristyn interrupted. "The peasants are going to clap their hands and Giselle will come out of that cottage!" She pointed to where the dancers had taken their positions. They clapped their hands and Kristyn waited, her eyes trained on the house. "She's missing the cue!" she whispered nervously to Hailey. "Where do you think she is?"

"I don't know," Hailey replied. "Back at the costume shop?"

The peasants clapped their hands again. Kristyn held her breath. She'd never seen a lead role miss a cue before. Where could Giselle be?

Suddenly, the door to the cottage opened

and Giselle's mother peered out, confused. She spotted Kristyn and waved her over. "Pssst! Giselle!" she called.

Kristyn looked around, shocked. "Who's she talking to?" she asked Hailey.

Hailey raised an unsure eyebrow. "I think she's talking to you," she whispered out of the side of her mouth.

"Me?" Kristyn exclaimed, her jaw dropping. "I'm not Giselle!"

Hailey pointed to Kristyn's costume. "You've got the dress and the hair and a new pair of—"

The friends exchanged a look and glanced down at Kristyn's pink feet. "Shoes!" they cried in unison.

The peasants clapped one more time, giving Kristyn her cue again.

"Dance now, ask questions later!" shouted Hailey, nudging Kristyn toward the gathering.

The music rose. Kristyn took her place in the circle and began to sway.

Hailey looked on proudly as Kristyn danced Giselle. There was no doubt about it: Kristyn's dancing was magical! Suddenly, Hailey spied Albrecht, the prince. He was disguised as a peasant and was watching Kristyn dance, mesmerized. Hailey put her hands on her hips. She knew how this story went. If Kristyn really was Giselle now, there was no way Hailey was letting slimy Albrecht get near her and break her heart! She marched in his direction.

"She's so beautiful," Albrecht sighed dreamily. "I must have her as my wife."

Hailey folded her arms across her chest. "So, you're a peasant, huh?" she said, eyeing him suspiciously.

Albrecht glanced sideways at her. "What?" he mumbled. "Yes. That's correct."

"Single, are you? No fiancée?" Hailey continued, remembering from the ballet that Albrecht was already engaged to marry a royal.

"No, of course not," Albrecht lied.

"Not masquerading as a peasant to deceive Giselle into marrying you?" Hailey pressed, narrowing her eyes. No way was she letting him get away with this!

Albrecht looked uncomfortable. "I wouldn't know what you're talking about," he said haughtily.

This guy is good, Hailey thought. Time to change tactics. "Caviar or beef stew?" she asked quickly.

"The caviar, of course," Albrecht answered.

"Aha!" Hailey shouted, pointing. Only a true aristocrat—or prince—would choose to eat caviar. Busted.

Kristyn ended her performance with a delicate arabesque and grinned. Dancing the part of Giselle felt as wonderful as she'd always imagined it would.

The group of peasants applauded, and Hailey

rushed to her side. "That was awesome!" she said, tugging Kristyn's arm. "Now let's get out of here!"

But Kristyn was still caught up in the moment. "These shoes! I love these shoes!" She wrestled her arm free from Hailey and pirouetted in a circle.

Suddenly, Albrecht appeared behind her. "My darling," he cooed. "You are more beautiful today than ever before."

Kristyn jumped, surprised. "Um . . . thank you?" she replied unsurely.

"Your eyes, blue as the sky, your hair, kissed with strawberry."

"Oh, yeah, right," replied Kristyn, playing along. She touched a lock of her hair. "I don't know why I didn't do this earlier."

"And I've never seen you dance like that before . . . or anyone else, for that matter," Albrecht continued, batting his eyelashes at Kristyn.

Kristyn blushed. She could get used to this kind of treatment!

Then another man, dressed in hunting attire, popped up behind her. *Why does this keep happening to me?* Kristyn thought.

"Giselle, this man is an impostor! Just look at his soft hands—not a day's hard work in his life!" declared the second man, pointing a finger at Albrecht.

Kristyn knew from the ballet that the second man was Hilarion, the hunter. In the story, every move Hilarion made was out of love for Giselle. He longed to prove that Albrecht was a phony and claim Giselle as his own true love.

Hilarion grabbed Albrecht's palms and flipped them over for her to inspect. "See? Feel how soft!" he cried.

Kristyn hesitated and then touched Albrecht's palm with one finger. Soft as a baby's bottom, she had to admit.

Albrecht yanked back his hands and looked smug. "It's true!" he confessed, throwing his arms in the air. "I'm royal. And rich. And stunning. Is any of that my fault?" He pulled a nearby daisy from the ground and dropped to his knee. He offered Kristyn the flower. "Providence shines down upon you today as I give you the honor of accepting my proposal."

Kristyn looked uncomfortable. *Proposal?* "I think there's been a little misunderstanding—" she started.

Now it was Hilarion's turn to look smug. "Exactly," he proclaimed. "Hello? Giselle and I are to be married tomorrow." He fell to his own knee next to Albrecht.

Kristyn looked at the two men kneeling before her. She wanted to dance—not get married! "Ha," she laughed nervously. "That's hilarious. You can get up now."

Albrecht scowled at Hilarion. "You? What can you offer her?" he sneered. "I am descended from the most royal of royal lineages. You are nothing but an oafish farm boy."

Hilarion puffed out his chest. "I am a hunter," he declared. "And a provider for this entire village." He fixed his gaze on Kristyn. "Giselle and I milked our first cows together. Remember, Giselle? I got you your first bucket."

"Bucket?" Kristyn wrung her hands. This was getting out of control. Did these guys really believe she was Giselle?

"Bucket!" Albrecht scoffed. "I can give her gold buckets, to carry her gold bullions in!"

"Hold on!" Kristyn cried, putting her hands out in front of her. "I'm *not* getting married. I'm only seventeen! Couldn't we just dance some more?"

Just then, Hailey interrupted. "Er, Giselle? A word?" She pulled Kristyn away from the boys, who were still arguing over who would make the better husband.

"Kristyn," Hailey said seriously. "We've got to get out of here."

Kristyn looked from Hailey to the boys and back again. "I don't know," she said giddily. "They're both kind of cute. And you saw me dance, right?"

Hailey gripped Kristyn's shoulders solemnly. "If this *is Giselle,* you know how this story ends, right?" Hailey grabbed her own hair and crossed her eyes. "Mad scene, dance, dance, sword in the heart." She staggered and pretended to stab herself. "Blah, blah, ghosts," she continued, flapping her arms like a ghost. "Wooo, wooo, white dress—grave," Hailey finished, collapsing dramatically on the ground.

Kristyn pursed her lips. Hailey had a point. "Yeah, it doesn't end well, does it?" she admitted. But still, they had only just gotten here. Surely she had a little more time before things got ugly. "Just one more dance?" she pleaded. "Then we'll go."

Hailey looked resigned. She eyed the boys, who were now wrestling each other on the ground. "They're busy. Let's go now," she suggested.

The girls slipped between two trees and were gone.

Chapter 6

"Where are we going?" Kristyn asked as she and Hailey made their way down a dusty, abandoned path.

"Anywhere but here," Hailey said anxiously.

Kristyn glanced around uneasily. She had to agree: something didn't feel right, but she couldn't put her finger on it. She shivered as a cold breeze blew through the trees.

Suddenly, the girls heard a rumbling on the path behind them. Kristyn turned around. In the distance, a snowy cloud was moving toward them. As it approached, she could make out a chariot and some reindeer. "Someone's coming," she whispered to Hailey. "Maybe they can give us a ride!" Kristyn stepped into the middle of the path and waved at the carriage.

"What are you doing?" Hailey asked frantically.

"Flagging down whoever is in that—"

"No, you're not!" Hailey cried. She dragged Kristyn into the bushes just as a huge crystal chariot thundered past.

The chariot skidded to a halt and turned sharply into the thicket.

"Wow, did you feel that?" Kristyn whispered to Hailey, shuddering against the sudden chill in the air.

"I d-d-d-did," Hailey said through chattering teeth.

"Who is that?"

Hailey wrapped her arms around herself. "Not anybody we need to meet!"

But Kristyn was curious. She darted down the path and peered through the foliage. Hailey followed her reluctantly.

"The Snow Queen," Kristyn whispered. She pointed toward the crystal chariot now parked in front of the peasants' houses. A woman with white hair and a majestic silver crystal dress sat atop the chariot, gripping the reins. She held her nose high in the air. There was a trail of ice behind the chariot, and the space around her was dotted with snowflakes. Kristyn watched wide-eyed as the Queen descended regally from her wintry ride.

Out in the clearing, all the peasants stopped in their tracks—all except for Albrecht and Hilarion. They were still fighting on the ground, completely oblivious to the sudden frost in the air.

"This is not over!" Hilarion shouted. "You can't just take whatever you want, everywhere you go!"

"Yes, I can!" Albrecht yelled, shoving Hilarion off of him. "I am sixth in line to the throne. Third, if you don't include my sisters, which I don't!"

The Queen cleared her throat. "Ahem," she said, frost escaping her mouth as she spoke.

Hilarion and Albrecht snapped suddenly to

attention. They joined the other peasants in a deep bow of respect.

Kristyn watched the Queen carefully. Something didn't add up. "What is she doing in *Giselle?*" she asked. The two ballets should have been totally separate. *Strange.*

"*That's* what bothers you most about this scenario?" Hailey remarked.

Kristyn turned her attention back to the clearing.

"Exactly *what* is happening here?" the Queen asked, looming over Albrecht and Hilarion.

"Uh . . . making plans for my wedding to Giselle, Majesty," Hilarion replied anxiously.

"He hopes in vain," Albrecht said. "Your Majesty will be the guest of honor at *my* wedding to Giselle."

The Snow Queen looked down her nose at the two men. "And where is the bride? Bring her here so I may watch her choose between you."

Hilarion and Albrecht looked around the clearing. They appeared frantic and frightened.

Kristyn ducked farther into the bushes. She looked worriedly at Hailey.

Hailey put her finger in front of her nose to stifle a sneeze. Kristyn winced. Now was not the time to blow their cover. Hailey gave a thumbs-up to let Kristyn know the sneeze had passed. Phew. That was close.

"I'm waiting!" called the Snow Queen.

Albrecht composed himself and took a timid step forward. "Your Majesty," he began. "If we had known you were coming, we could have—"

"Giselle is gone, ma'am," Hilarion finished.

"Gone? Gone where?" the Queen demanded. Giselle did not have her permission to just *disappear*. That was not the way the story went. Something had to be done.

The Queen frostily scanned the area with her icy glare. "How did this happen?" she insisted.

"I fear that she is not entirely well," Hilarion bluffed.

"Go on," commanded the Queen.

"He's right for once, Your Majesty," continued Albrecht, going along with it. "She was not quite herself today. She spoke of . . . not wanting to marry me."

The Queen swept her arm, sending a blast of arctic air toward them. "Silence!" she proclaimed.

In the bushes, Kristyn wrung her hands. "Wow. I got them in trouble by leaving," she said. It hadn't occurred to her that her presence might cause problems for the others who were already living in this strange ballet world. Kristyn had only wanted to explore. But by the looks of things, the Queen was not happy to have her order disrupted. Kristyn stood and brushed off her dress. "I'll just go and explain, and we'll all have a big laugh."

Hailey yanked her back behind the bushes. "Do you see *them* laughing?"

Kristyn paused and then shook her head. Once again, Hailey had a point.

Back in the clearing, the Snow Queen was still looking for answers. "Did anyone else see anything?"

One of the peasants stepped forward. "She

was wearing pink shoes," the woman volunteered in a small voice.

The crowd nodded in agreement behind her.

"It's true," Hilarion stated. "She wore beautiful pink shoes."

The Snow Queen marched toward Giselle's mother. "Where did she get pink shoes?" she demanded.

Giselle's mother cowered. "From Claude?" she replied. "The cobbler?"

"That is not the answer I was looking for." The Snow Queen blew a frigid blast of air over the woman, freezing her in place. Then she climbed aboard her icy chariot. "Find her," she commanded. "I will *not* tolerate this kind of disruption."

Albrecht bowed deeply. "Of course, Your Majesty."

"I will leave no stone unturned," Hilarion declared, making a break for his horse.

"Led by me," Albrecht called, racing to his own horse.

"Until then, dance!" the Queen commanded

the peasants. "Go! Be perrrrfect!"

The peasants laughed nervously but did not dare move.

"What are you waiting for?" the Queen cried.

The peasants looked at one another and began to move in time to the *Giselle* music now playing.

The Snow Queen cracked her whip and drove out of the glade, freezing flowers, leaves, and trees as she passed.

Kristyn glanced at Hailey. She hadn't meant to get anyone in trouble. But now she felt responsible for making sure this situation didn't get worse. "We have to do something," she said anxiously. "I can be Giselle for a little while longer."

Hailey knitted her eyebrows together in concern. "For how long?" she asked. "Until you go mad or until you're a ghost?"

They looked toward the peasants, who were busy moving Giselle's frozen mother in front of her house.

"It's not safe here," Hailey continued. "We

have to go." She pulled Kristyn out of the bushes and back onto the path leading away from the glade.

Kristyn gave a final glance over her shoulder.

Suddenly, they heard the sound of horse hooves. They turned in time to see Prince Albrecht and Hilarion racing toward them. They ducked behind a bush until the boys had passed. Now what?

Hailey crossed her arms, pointing each hand in a different direction. "Madame Frosty went that way. The Goofy Brothers went that way." She pointed straight ahead, deciding. "Let's go this way."

Chapter 7

"I don't see anything that looks like a way home," Kristyn remarked as she and Hailey continued walking. She had no idea how they had even gotten there, much less how they were supposed to get home.

"I don't either," Hailey answered.

"Maybe we should go back the way we came. That would be logical," Kristyn suggested.

Hailey threw up her hands. "Logical?" she cried. "Either we're dreaming the same dream, or somehow we've landed in a crazy time-warp ballet world!"

Kristyn had to admit Hailey was right. This adventure was turning out to be anything but logical. Still, she wasn't sure she wanted to return to regular life just yet. "All I know is I danced Giselle! And the steps were 'perrrrfect' if I do say so myself."

Hailey arched her eyebrow. "Again, does that sound logical?"

But Kristyn's head was in the clouds. "When we get home, I want Madame Katerina to order me ten pairs of these shoes," she sang, twirling as she walked.

Hailey stopped short. "The shoes! It has to be the shoes." She bent down in front of Kristyn and started untying the bright pink ribbons.

"What are you doing?" Kristyn cried, jumping out of Hailey's reach.

"You put on the shoes and—*poof!*—we're here in this wacky land. So, if you take them off . . . ," she reasoned, lunging for Kristyn's ankles again.

"No way!" Kristyn shouted. "I'm not taking off these shoes!" She ran farther down the path, which was difficult with one half-untied toe shoe. She hobbled into a thicket of trees and fixed her ribbons, Hailey's voice fading behind her.

"It makes sense! Listen! Wait!" Hailey

popped her head through the branches. "Can't we just try to—"

The girls skidded to a halt. They were standing at the edge of a pristine, brilliant lake. The sun was setting in the distance, its rays shimmering on the surface of the water. The colors of the trees around them were the fiery hues of fall: orange, red, and yellow. Everything was bathed in soft, golden light.

"Whoa," Hailey said under her breath.

"Exactly," Kristyn replied dreamily. It was the most spectacular setting she had ever seen.

"I mean, whoa, check *yourself* out!" Hailey cried.

Kristyn snapped to attention and looked at Hailey, whose eyes were practically bugging out of her head. Kristyn bent to see her own reflection in the glassy water.

"Double whoa," she said as she touched her hair. Her strawberry blond Giselle locks and blue dress were gone. Kristyn was now a brunette. She smoothed her hand over the spectacular white tutu she was suddenly wearing.

Hailey pointed across the lake. "Swans!" Hailey exclaimed.

Kristyn followed her gaze and saw a group of beautiful white birds gliding along the water's surface. It was a stunning scene. "Swans," Kristyn repeated. "On the lake?" *Swan Lake* was only Kristyn's favorite ballet of all time.

Hailey put her arms out in front of her. "Let's not overreact," she replied. "Every time you find migratory fowl on a body of water doesn't mean you have . . ."

Her voice trailed away as the sun slipped below the horizon. A few of the swans swam to the edge of the lake and stepped out onto dry land.

Kristyn watched, mouth open, as the birds changed into beautiful dancers while the moon rose slowly. Just like in the ballet! Kristyn recognized their classic *Swan Lake* tutus.

Hailey put her hands on her hips. "Okay, that's pretty much your basic *Swan Lake*," she announced matter-of-factly.

Kristyn couldn't hide her grin. This dream—

time warp—whatever-it-was—just kept getting better and better! First *Giselle* and now *Swan Lake*. She couldn't wait to see what happened next!

Chapter 8

The Snow Queen and her traveling snowstorm stopped in their tracks. They had come across a Nutcracker and a Sugar Plum Fairy.

The Snow Queen marched in front of them, barking orders. "You will inspect every doghouse, mouse house, and gingerbread house in the land until Giselle is found and brought to me. Do I make myself clear?"

"Y-y-yes, Your Majesty," the Nutcracker stuttered nervously.

The Sugar Plum Fairy raised her hand. "Gone?" she asked in a squeaky voice. "Just, like, gone? *Poof?* Wearing pink shoes? Oooh! Sounds exciting!" she exclaimed, jumping up and down.

The Snow Queen blew a chilly blast of air her way. The fairy froze mid-jump, a look of horror etched on her face. The Snow Queen smiled cruelly. "Anyone else craving excitement?" she challenged.

The Nutcracker silently shook his head. Nope!

Meanwhile, at the lake, Kristyn and Hailey looked on as the swans continued their transformation from birds to dancers.

One of the dancers waved her arm at Kristyn. "Odette! Hello, Odette! Here's your crown!"

The dancer reached into the nook of a tree and retrieved a sparkling tiara.

Kristyn's mouth dropped open. The tiara looked just like the one she had admired in Madame Katerina's costume shop.

The dancer offered Kristyn the crown. Kristyn placed it carefully on her head and leaned toward Hailey, cupping her hand to whisper, "They think I'm Odette." She smiled as she said the words. "The Swan Queen."

Hailey pointed a nervous finger at Kristyn. "We can't get involved here," she warned.

Kristyn ignored her and pointed to her own head. "Did you see the crown?" she asked excitedly.

Hailey rolled her eyes. "Kristyn, I *made* the crown," she reminded her friend. She reached for it to examine it more closely. "Although," she said, eyeing the jewels and tapping the frame, "this one looks real!"

Kristyn clapped her hands. "You're finally catching on, Hailey! This whole thing is real." She gestured behind her at the dancers. "These poor girls have been turned into swans by the evil sorcerer Rothbart."

"I know the story," Hailey replied, crossing her arms.

"And this lake is made of their parents' tears," Kristyn continued.

Hailey wrinkled her nose. "Ew!" she cried. "Lake of Parents' Tears? How did I miss that part?" She trained her eyes on Kristyn. "Look," she said sternly. "Just give them back their crown

Kristyn is a dancer who dreams of being
the prima ballerina.

Madame Katerina finds Kristyn a pair of
pink ballet shoes.

Kristyn's new shoes are magical! They whisk Kristyn and
her friend Hailey away to a dream ballet world.

Kristyn's favorite ballet comes to life—and she is
the lead dancer!

Kristyn and Hailey hide when
the evil Snow Queen arrives.

Kristyn's outfit magically transforms as she enters
the ballet *Swan Lake*.

Kristyn is crowned Odette, the Swan Queen.

Kristyn and Prince Siegfried dance
beautifully together.

The evil magician Rothbart turns Kristyn
and Hailey into swans!

Rothbart introduces his daughter Odile, transformed
to look like Odette, to Prince Siegfried.

Kristyn and Hailey interrupt Odile's dance
with the prince—and break the spell!

Odile looks on angrily as Kristyn dances
with the prince.

 Oh, no—the Snow Queen has captured Hailey!
Kristyn and her new friends hurry to the
Snow Queen's palace.

Kristyn fights the Snow Queen's icy magic
and rescues Hailey!

Kristyn takes off her shoes so that she and Hailey can go home.

Kristyn dances from her heart and earns the lead role in a new ballet!

and let's go. Don't even think about dancing."

"Okay . . . ," Kristyn started.

Just then, from the other side of the thicket, a handsome young man appeared. Kristyn did a double take. Was it just her or did this guy look like Dillon?

The man walked toward them. He was carrying a bow and arrow, and he looked even more striking bathed in moonlight.

"Prince Siegfried," Kristyn said in awe, remembering him from the ballet.

"Of course," Hailey said, letting out a sigh.

Siegfried approached and took Kristyn's hand. "Good evening, ladies," he said in a deep voice. He addressed the group but kept his eyes locked on Kristyn. "I'm most fortunate to come upon such beauty here in the moonlight. My name is Siegfried."

Kristyn stared deep into the prince's eyes. "You look so familiar," she said dreamily.

"I'm a prince. I get that a lot," replied Siegfried. "And what are your names?"

Kristyn gestured to Hailey. "This is my

friend Hailey. And my name is"—she paused— "Odette. My name is Odette."

Hailey slapped her palm on her forehead. "Oy!" she exclaimed. It looked like they were going to be here awhile.

Just then, the music rose, as if from the lake. Kristyn recognized it instantly. She and Siegfried took their positions and began to dance a pas de deux. Kristyn could hardly contain her excitement. It was just like how it happened onstage! Only this time *she*—not Tara—was dancing the lead. The group of swan dancers swayed in time to the music behind them as Hailey looked on.

"Odette, do you live nearby?" Siegfried questioned as they performed a complicated series of spins.

Kristyn bit her lip. *How to explain?* "I'm from, you know, around."

As they moved through their routine, Kristyn felt a familiar surge of joy. The music flowed through her veins and made her feel alive. She began to add a few steps of her own to the dance. To her surprise, Siegfried followed her lead and kept pace with her, improvising along the way.

Kristyn beamed. This was even better than a dream!

As Kristyn was dancing, the branches parted across the thicket. A sinister-looking man peered through the gap. If Kristyn could have seen him, she would have recognized him as the evil Rothbart. He looked strangely like Mr. Pennington. A cloud of suspicion crossed Rothbart's face. "So," he hissed, "little Miss Odette has come to the party."

"Wow!" Siegfried exclaimed. "I've never seen anyone dance like this! It's like you're making up the steps as you go along."

Kristyn grinned. "It just flows right through

me," she replied. Kristyn and Siegfried gazed dreamily into each other's eyes. The crowd of swans around them applauded.

Siegfried pulled Kristyn closer to him. "I know we just met," he said softly. "But I want to invite you to a party tomorrow night. I want you to know more about my world."

Kristyn considered Siegfried's offer. She knew Hailey wouldn't like it, but she couldn't pass up the opportunity to remain Odette for just a little while longer. Besides, it wasn't every day that a prince invited her to a party at his castle! "I could stay here forever," she said, almost to herself.

"I hope you do," Siegfried replied.

Still hidden in the thicket, Rothbart thought about Kristyn and Siegfried's conversation. "'Stay here forever,' eh? Oh, you will," he snickered evilly. "Right here on this lake!"

Chapter 9

"Kristyn!" Hailey shouted.

The light of dawn started to creep through the tree leaves above them. They had been in the forest all night! According to Rothbart's curse, morning light meant the swans were once again confined to the lake. As if on cue, the dancers moved toward the water as the sun rose over the hill.

Kristyn, still by Siegfried's side, heard her friend calling her. "I think it might be time for me to go now," she mumbled sadly.

Siegfried clasped both her hands. "Say you'll come to the party? I won't leave until you say yes." Kristyn glanced over her shoulder at Hailey. Hailey made her arms look like the hands of a clock, tick-tocking away. *Time to go.*

Kristyn felt conflicted. She knew that if she said yes, she'd be making a promise to Siegfried that she couldn't keep. But she also knew she didn't want this beautiful moment to end.

"I'll be there," she declared, before she let herself think about it for too long. "Save a dance for me."

"I will only dance with you," Siegfried replied. He kissed her hand. "Until then."

Kristyn held her hand to her heart and watched him leave through a hole in the trees. Wistfully, she turned toward Hailey. "Isn't he dreamy?" she gushed.

"Uh, yes," Hailey replied hastily. "But we need to go!"

"But what about the party?" Kristyn asked.

"Aren't you forgetting what Rothbart does to Odette?" Hailey nervously tugged on Kristyn's arm. "Magic spell, turn into swan, tragic ending— remember?"

Just then, a sinister voice spoke. "Thank you for that flattering introduction," the voice said. "Too late."

"Rothbart!" Hailey and Kristyn exclaimed as the villain emerged from the thicket. The sorcerer stretched out his hands, shooting an evil spell toward the girls.

"Shoes, Kristyn!" Hailey shouted. "It's our only chance. Take off those pink—"

But Rothbart's spell worked too quickly. Dark magic swirled around them, wrapping them in a fog.

Horrified, Kristyn watched as her feet turned bright pink and became webbed. They were the feet of a swan.

"Gaaahhhh!" Kristyn and Hailey both shouted. "You're a—" They each pointed a finger at the other. They were both covered with feathers! Just like the dancers, they were now bound to the lake by Rothbart's curse.

"This is so not my day," Hailey proclaimed.

Kristyn hung her head. This was all her fault.

Rothbart laughed meanly. "Now my darling daughter, Odile, will marry Prince Siegfried, without so much as a honk from any of you. Do you understand?"

Kristyn had forgotten this part of the story. Rothbart wished for his own daughter to marry Siegfried. That way Rothbart would have the power of the royal family on his side. The only thing standing in the way of his plan was Odette. Or in this case, Kristyn. Yikes.

Suddenly, Rothbart lunged toward Kristyn. She swerved, causing her crown to fly off into the bushes.

Hailey flapped her wings and pecked at Rothbart's feet, trying to protect her friend.

"Ahhh!" Rothbart cried.

Kristyn dove for the water and turned to see Rothbart grab Hailey by the neck. "Peck him!" Kristyn shouted. "Flap! Peck at his shoes!"

Hailey nodded and let out a loud honk.

Rothbart looked down and gasped. "Ahhh! My new shoes!"

"Now get in the water!" Kristyn hollered.

Hailey scrambled to the water's edge and dipped a toe in. "Lake of tears! Ick! Icky! Gross!" she cried. She yanked out her foot, flapping her wings hysterically.

Just then, an icy blast ripped through the clearing, knocking Rothbart to the ground.

That frigid air meant only one thing: the Snow Queen. Kristyn swam to shore and huddled against Hailey.

Seconds later, the Queen's crystal chariot skidded to a halt in front of the sorcerer.

She sure knows how to make an entrance, thought Kristyn, flapping her wings for warmth.

Out on the water, the other swans clustered together.

"Rothbart," the Snow Queen bellowed from her perch. "Rebellion is spreading across the land. What news?"

Rebellion? Kristyn thought. *She can't mean me! All I wanted to do was dance!*

"Not a problem here. Everything is fine," Rothbart replied shakily from the ground. He reached nervously into his backpack. "Er . . . pheasant jerky? Quail jerky? Swan jerky?" he offered.

The Snow Queen eyed him suspiciously.

Kristyn shook her wings with determination.

She had to get them out of this situation alive. "Act natural," she instructed Hailey. "Do something swan-ish," she said, pecking the ground with her swan beak.

Hailey nodded. She began honking loudly and flapped noisily around in a circle.

Kristyn grimaced. Leave it to Hailey to go all out! "Okay," she revised. "Now do half as much."

The girls watched as Rothbart struggled to his feet. He wiped his forehead with his cape and cleared his throat, trying to regain his composure.

"So, Your Majesty," the evil sorcerer said. "As you can see, everything is hunky-dory." He began coughing uncontrollably.

The Snow Queen considered him carefully. "You will attend the prince's Regency Ball, I presume," she said.

"Of course," Rothbart replied, bowing deeply. "With my little flower, Odile. She grows more beautiful and talented by the day. She will be honored to dance for the prince."

"Yes, as she must," the Snow Queen said. With a quick snap of her reins she was gone, taking her icy air with her.

Rothbart breathed a loud sigh of relief and turned toward the swans. "I'm off to the ball," he announced, "where they'll be serving roast swan livers!" He pointed toward Kristyn. Then he spun on his heel and marched into the forest.

Chapter 10

Kristyn took a deep breath. This dreamy ballet world suddenly had some pretty real dangers. First the Snow Queen and now Rothbart—as if one villain weren't bad enough.

"What are we going to do now?" Hailey asked, giving her feathers a good shake.

Kristyn tilted her head, considering their options. After a pause, she said, "There's only one place we can go."

"And that is?" Hailey prompted.

Kristyn stretched her long swan neck in the direction of Siegfried's castle. "To the ball!" she cried. "I have to dance with Siegfried again in order to break Rothbart's spell."

Hailey rolled her eyes. This was getting ridiculous. "The only thing that can break the spell is *true love*. You only danced with him *once*."

Kristyn got a faraway look in her eyes. "Yes," she murmured. "But there was magic in the air. Didn't you feel it?"

"Yes, there was magic in the air," Hailey replied sarcastically. "From Rothbart. And now we're *swans*!"

Kristyn put a wing around her best friend. Hailey was right. Things definitely hadn't gone according to plan. But Kristyn also knew what would happen if they quit now. "We have to get to the ball before Rothbart's daughter, Odile, can trick the prince into saying he loves *her* instead." The way she saw it, dancing at the ball was their only way out. That is, unless they wanted to wear feathers for life.

Hailey sighed. She looked at the castle in the distance. "It's going to be a long walk with these tiny feet," she said, pointing to their webbed swan toes.

"But Hailey, we've got these!" Kristyn cried, flapping her wings excitedly. "How hard can it be?" To prove her point, Kristyn ducked her head and took off running. She opened her wings and glided into the air. She flew low at first but then flapped faster, soaring high into the sky. She looped over the lake and circled back toward Hailey.

As she came in for the landing, she put her feet out to stop herself. Skidding to an ungraceful halt, she laughed. "That was amazing!" she exclaimed, taking off again. "I'm flying! Try it!"

"Sure, how hard can it be?" Hailey muttered unsurely. She got a running start, waved her wings furiously and felt herself lift an inch off the ground. But she forgot to keep flapping and— *crash!*—landed with a thud. Hailey groaned. Coordination just wasn't her thing! "I can't do it," she called.

"Keep trying," Kristyn encouraged her from far above.

But Hailey didn't want to keep trying. Exhausted, she plopped down on the ground, and her eyes filled with tears. It had been such a long day already, full of too much drama. A sad little *honk* escaped her beak.

Kristyn flew down next to Hailey and wrapped her wing around her. "I'm sorry we're in this mess, Hail," she said sincerely. After all, it was her fault they were learning to fly in the first place. Maybe it had been a little selfish, insisting that they stay here so long—even if Kristyn was getting to live some of her dream. Seeing Hailey so upset, Kristyn suddenly didn't feel it was worth it.

Kristyn sighed. She wasn't exactly sure how they were going to get out of this mess but she did know one thing: they'd do it together. She squeezed Hailey into a bear hug. "We'll get back! We're best friends, and we can do this!" She raised her wing toward Hailey in a high five.

Hailey gave a small smile and raised her own wing to Kristyn's. "Okay. I'll try it again." She stood up, shook out her feathers, and prepared for battle. But then she stopped and motioned to Kristyn.

Was that singing she heard?

Kristyn and Hailey peered across the clearing. Hilarion and Albrecht approached on horseback, singing in unison. They paused at the lake's shimmering edge.

Hilarion reached into his satchel and pulled out some bread and fruit. He shared it with the prince as they admired the scenery. Apparently, the two had called a truce.

"Hey! It's the wedding singers," Hailey cried. "And they've got some food." She waddled toward the guys, honking and flapping her wings. She was famished!

"Be careful!" Kristyn cried, following her.

"Pah! We're just birds, remember?" Hailey said. She honked and marched in front of Hilarion.

Hilarion broke off a crust of bread and tossed it toward her. "Look at the plump swans," he said as Hailey gobbled up the morsel.

"Plump? Why, you . . ." Hailey rushed toward Hilarion, insulted and honking furiously.

The hunter reached swiftly into his pack and pulled out his bow and arrow. He aimed it squarely at the girls.

"Hailey!" Kristyn squawked.

Hilarion steadied his aim. "I'll bag a few for Giselle!" he proclaimed.

"Fly, Hailey, fly!" Kristyn urged.

"Oh, boy," Hailey breathed. All she'd wanted was a little snack!

Albrecht grabbed the bow from Hilarion and took aim himself. "Allow me!"

Hailey beat her wings and prepared to take off. With all her might she threw her body forward and glided into the air—just as an arrow landed in the tree right behind her. *Thwack!*

"You did it!" Kristyn exclaimed.

"I can fly!" Hailey squealed.

The girls took off through the air in the direction of Siegfried's castle.

Chapter 11

That evening, Rothbart and his daughter, Odile, approached the castle.

"How do I look, Daddy?" Odile asked, smoothing her swan costume.

"Perfect," the sorcerer replied. "Except for one thing." He waved a hand over his daughter's head. Magic swirled around her, transforming her into the spitting image of Odette. The only thing missing was the pair of pink toe shoes that Kristyn wore. Odile's toe shoes were black.

"Perfect," Rothbart said, admiring his handiwork. "Now go. Get him to say he loves you, and Odette will remain a swan forever!"

Odile spun around. "I'm ready for my close-up," she announced as the pair glided through the palace gate.

In the ballroom, Siegfried and his mother waited for guests to arrive.

When Odile entered, dressed perfectly as Odette, Siegfried gasped. "There she is," he said, nudging his mother. "The girl I've been telling you about."

Queen Vera nodded her head in approval. She wanted Prince Siegfried to choose a bride that evening. "She's lovely, my dear."

"I think she's the one." Siegfried sighed as Odile and her father approached.

Rothbart bowed deeply in a show of respect for the Queen. "Your Majesty," he said, sweeping his arm toward Odile. "Allow me to introduce my daughter."

Odile curtsied gracefully.

Siegfried grasped her hands. "Odette, I'm so glad you are here. Shall we dance?" he asked, leading her toward the ballroom.

"Are you ready to make magic?" Odile cooed.

The orchestra played, and the pair swirled around the dance floor.

To an outsider, their moves appeared flawless. But to Siegfried, something didn't feel right. The steps didn't come as easily as they had before. "I'm sorry," he apologized. "I guess I'm just a little off."

Odile smiled slyly. The plan was in motion.

Kristyn and Hailey fluttered through the sky toward the palace. They'd been in the air almost all day, and Kristyn had to admit it: she was beat!

"Wow," Hailey remarked. "We do *not* fly quickly. I did not know that about swans."

"I just hope we aren't late," Kristyn replied, flapping her wings a little faster.

The royal pavilion emerged in the distance, and the girls swooped down toward it. They skidded to a halt on the veranda. They could hear music playing inside.

"That music!" Kristyn cried, recognizing the

familiar *Swan Lake* tune. "They've started!" She waddled toward an open window and peered inside. Sure enough, Odile, disguised as Kristyn's Odette, was spinning around the ballroom with the prince.

"She's me already," Kristyn declared.

"And according to Rothbart's curse, you can't transform back into yourself until the sun sets again," Hailey reminded her.

Kristyn nodded. It would be difficult to convince Siegfried of the truth in her current swan body. She glanced toward the sun. It was inching closer toward the horizon. She poked her long neck through the window to get a better look at what was happening inside.

Kristyn watched as the prince and Odile grew closer and closer with each step. "Look how he's gazing into her eyes!" she cried. "He's totally falling for her—I mean me!" she sputtered, getting confused herself.

Then Kristyn spied Rothbart in the corner. He was watching his daughter and the prince with a satisfied sneer. Kristyn frowned. "We've got to stop those two!" she cried desperately.

The girls watched the sun slip closer and closer to the horizon. They still had a few minutes until they would turn into humans for the evening.

"We need a distraction until the sun goes down," Hailey said, putting on her game face.

What kind of distraction? Kristyn wondered. Suddenly, she had it. What better way to distract a ball then to send in a couple of wild swans? "C'mon!" Kristyn shouted to Hailey. She flapped her wings and leaped through the open window.

Hailey hesitated and then tumbled clumsily through the window after Kristyn. The girls spilled into the ballroom just as Prince Siegfried leaned toward Odile for a kiss.

Chapter 12

The crowd buzzed with surprise as the swans waddled across the floor.

"Oh, my!"

"Look!"

"Swans in the pavilion!"

"Take a gander at that!"

The girls raced around the ballroom floor, causing as big a commotion as they could muster. Kristyn looked over her wing at the sun falling halfway behind the hill. "Almost there," she called to Hailey. They just needed a little more time!

Hailey flapped her wings. *Honk! Honk!*

"Almost there," Kristyn repeated.

Then the last ray of sun dipped behind the hill and, just as the curse promised, a swirl of glittering magic instantly enveloped Kristyn. She changed from a swan back into beautiful Odette.

"Ahhh!" Hailey squawked as she transformed back into herself at the same time. She crashed into a table of refreshments.

Kristyn glided gracefully across the ballroom toward Odile and the prince. "Not so fast, prince stealer!" she announced.

Siegfried's mouth dropped open as he looked from Odile to Odette and back again, trying to make sense of it all. "What?" he cried, clearly confused by the two identical dancers.

The crowd gasped.

"Look! It's another Odette!"

"There are two of them!"

Kristyn locked eyes with Prince Siegfried. "What about that dance you promised?" she asked.

Odile placed a hand on the prince's arm. "Focus here, Siegfried. This is *my* dance."

Prince Siegfried furrowed his brow. He looked from Kristyn to Odile, trying to decide which was the real Odette.

"That pink-footed swan in the grass is about to ruin everything!" snarled Rothbart from the sidelines of the dance floor. "Keep dancing, Odette!" he called to his daughter.

Siegfried brought a hand to his forehead. "Which one of you is the girl I love?" he asked, exasperated.

"Can't you tell?" Odile replied slyly. "I'm the one who knows the moves," she said. As if to demonstrate, she leaped high into the air in a perfect grande jette from the second act of *Swan Lake*. Madame Natasha would have been proud.

"Ahhh," Kristyn replied. "You're going all Black Swan on me now, are you? Act two? No problem." Kristyn mimicked Odile's classical footwork, embellishing with her own moves as she went along.

Before he knew it, Siegfried was dancing a powerful pas de trois with both girls at once. He looked as if his head might start spinning right along with his feet!

Odile sashayed around the prince, whispering in his ear. "This isn't going to work. Right,

Siegfried? She's a fraud!" She executed a series of precise spins to prove her point.

Kristyn wasn't worried. She let the music take over and felt that familiar surge. She danced with emotion, adding her signature moves to the routine. *This ought to get his attention,* she thought.

Siegfried watched as Kristyn glided effortlessly across the ballroom floor. "It's all starting to come back to me," he said. He moved toward her.

Before Kristyn knew it, they were performing the same pas de deux they had begun the day before by the lake.

Odile frowned. She struggled to find some way back into the dance. But it was clear that this number only had room for two. "This isn't how it goes!" she squealed. "Those aren't the steps! What are you doing?"

"Something magical," Siegfried said in a dreamy voice.

Kristyn glanced over her shoulder at Odile. "You dance your way, I'll dance mine," she said, leaping into the air. Siegfried caught her, lifting her high above his head. He lowered her safely to the ground and gazed into her eyes.

"It's you," he murmured. "You're the one I love. Will you marry me?"

Kristyn felt the world around her stand still. "Why does everyone keep asking me that?" she joked.

"You're the one I've been looking for," he said.

"Looks like I got here just in time," she replied.

Behind her, Odile twirled dramatically in the air, trying desperately to capture Siegfried's attention once more. But with her eyes focused on the prince she didn't check her landing. *Crash!* She came down hard on her foot. *Riiiip!*

Uh-oh. Kristyn recognized that sound.

"Daddyyyy!" Odile wailed, clutching her ripped toe shoe and limping off the dance floor. Rothbart raced across the ballroom and scooped his daughter into his arms.

Odile scowled at him. "You said to trust you!

You said you had an eye for these things!"

"You're overwrought," Rothbart replied, whisking her toward the door. "Let's get you some fresh air."

Kristyn shook her head as Rothbart fled the ballroom with Odile. *Looks like their party is over,* she thought.

Meanwhile, on the sidelines, Hailey watched Kristyn and Siegfried reconnect. "Okay, Kristyn," she said under her breath. "Love, love, love. Spell is broken. Now let's get out of here before we break out in feathers again." But just as she was about to interrupt, Hailey felt a chilly blast whip around her.

"Oh, no," she muttered. An icy wind out of nowhere could only mean one thing: the Snow Queen.

Sure enough, the villainess appeared beside her. The Queen took in the scene through narrowed eyes.

"What have I missed?" she asked frostily. "Has Siegfried professed his love?"

"Y-y-yes," Hailey stammered, feeling frozen in place. She was soooo ready to get out of this place!

They watched as Siegfried escorted Kristyn to his mother's throne. Queen Vera hugged Kristyn tightly.

The Snow Queen eyed them suspiciously. "Something's not right here," she said. Then she fixed her glare on Hailey. "Who are you?"

"I'm Ha-ha-hailey," she replied, teeth chattering with cold.

The Snow Queen considered her. "You don't belong in this story."

No kidding, Hailey agreed. But what was the Snow Queen doing in *Swan Lake?*

On the throne, Queen Vera fawned over Kristyn's dress. "Your style is magnificent, Odette!" she exclaimed. "What a handsome couple you make. And that dancing!"

Kristyn blushed. "He really got his dance on!" she replied, poking Siegfried playfully.

Siegfried cocked his head, confused. "What is that? 'Got my dance on'?"

Kristyn grinned. "It just means that it's fun to take a few steps from your heart sometimes." She looked over her shoulder in search of Hailey. "You have to dance like nobody is watching."

"But in this world, somebody is always watching," Siegfried said somberly.

Kristyn shivered. Was it her or had an icy breeze just entered the room? But she shook off her feelings of dread when Siegfried took her hand. He pulled her onto the dance floor once more.

"Another chance to 'get my dance on,' my lady?"

Kristyn frowned, rethinking things. She wanted nothing more than to keep dancing. But she also knew that she hadn't been totally truthful with Siegfried. And if she continued to mislead him, then she was no better than Odile.

"Sorry, Siegfried. Not tonight. I have to tell you something."

Siegfried put a finger to his lips. "Shhh. Not before I ask you something." Siegfried got down on one knee and looked hopefully into Kristyn's eyes. "I love you, Odette. Will you be my wife?"

Before she could answer, another frigid blast of air swept through the room. Now Kristyn knew she wasn't imagining it. "The Snow Queen!" she exclaimed, searching the room for Hailey. But she still didn't see her best friend anywhere. Where was she? *Maybe she stepped outside,* Kristyn thought.

Lunging for the front door, Kristyn slipped and fell on a trail of slick ice leading right out of the pavilion. As she struggled to regain her footing, she spotted Hailey's sewing glasses—the ones she always carried in her apron pocket—on the floor in front of her. Hailey would never leave those behind on purpose. Kristyn put the pieces together. Icy trail plus glasses minus Hailey equaled only one thing: the Snow Queen had kidnapped her best friend!

"Hailey!" Kristyn shouted, scrambling to her feet and making her way back to Siegfried. "I don't have time to talk!" she gushed. "All I can tell you is that things are a huge mess right now, and I've got to go!"

Siegfried grabbed her hand, a look of concern in his eyes. "Go? Where? My guards can take you anywhere you need to go."

Kristyn shook her head. "I don't want anyone else getting hurt." She placed her hand gently on Siegfried's cheek. "Thank you for this, the dance, for everything." She turned on her heel and dashed from the pavilion, not daring to look back.

Chapter 13

Outside, the full moon shone brightly in the night sky. Its glow illuminated a path of ice leading north. *That must be the way the Snow Queen— and Hailey—went,* Kristyn reasoned. She spied a looming gray castle far in the distance. Its frosty façade gleamed in the moonlight. Kristyn made her way carefully along the frozen path.

"Hailey!" she called into the chilly night air. "Hailey!"

Listening to her voice echo across the icy forest, Kristyn suddenly felt hopeless. The castle was so far away! How would she get there in time? It was the middle of the night and she was already freezing. Not to mention her heart ached from leaving Siegfried. *Hailey wouldn't even be in this mess if it weren't for me,* Kristyn thought.

What kind of best friend am I? She sank to the ground beside the road and put her face in her hands. Then she began to cry.

A few minutes later, Kristyn heard the clip-clopping of horse hoofs, followed by voices. It was Hilarion and Prince Albrecht! They were still looking for Giselle.

Kristyn leaped to her feet and dusted off her swan costume. She ran down the road toward the two men. "Hey!" she shouted, waving her arms frantically. "I'm here!"

Albrecht spied her and pointed. "There she is!" he cried.

Hilarion followed Albrecht's gaze. He peered at her through the darkness. "The hair?" he said suspiciously, eyeing Kristyn's dark locks. She didn't have Giselle's strawberry blond locks or blue dress anymore. It was no wonder Hilarion didn't recognize her.

But then Albrecht pointed at Kristyn's familiar pink toe shoes. "The shoes!" he exclaimed.

Hilarion nodded, and they both scrambled to dismount.

"Miss," Hilarion called. "May we be of some assistance?"

"Oh, thank goodness it's you guys," Kristyn said with a relieved sigh.

"Giselle?" Hilarion questioned, upon hearing her voice. "Is that you?"

Kristyń bit her lip. How could she possibly explain her evening? Albrecht and Hilarion would never understand—she could hardly wrap her mind around it herself. "Oh, yeah," she replied, giving up. "Giselle, right. Listen, the Snow Queen kidnapped my best friend and took her away!"

But Hilarion was still puzzled. "But you look so different from before."

Albrecht interrupted. "Marry me!" he said, stepping in front of Hilarion.

"No, me!" Hilarion declared, shoving Albrecht to the side.

"Stop!" Kristyn cried, putting up her hands. What was it with guys around here? All this talk about weddings and marriage was starting to give her a headache. "I like a nice wedding as much as the next person, but—"

Hilarion and Albrecht looked confused.

Kristyn closed her eyes. She needed to think. "Please," she said after a long pause. "Just take me to the Snow Queen's palace. I have to get my friend."

Hilarion raised an eyebrow. "And take on the Snow Queen by yourself?"

Kristyn took a deep breath. "I don't think things will get that far," she said, though she wasn't really sure what to expect. "We just have to find Hailey. Who's with me?" She marched over to Hilarion's horse and wedged her foot into one of the stirrups.

Kristyn counted to three and swung her leg wildly over the saddle. "Whooooa!" she cried, flailing her arms as she went sailing right over the horse. *Thud!* She landed on the ground on the other side.

Hilarion and Albrecht scrambled to help her to her feet.

"I'm good," she mumbled, cheeks burning.

A few moments later, Kristyn was riding

with Albrecht on his trusty mare, his warm cape wrapped around her shoulders. Hilarion followed behind them on his own horse. The air seemed to grow even more frigid the closer they got to the castle.

They steered their horses around a corner and paused. The ice queen's palace loomed before them. It was even more menacing up close.

Kristyn shivered. "Whoa." She exhaled, taking it all in. "What goes on in there?"

Albrecht patted his nervous horse's neck to calm it. "I've only heard stories," he replied. "None of them good." He snapped his reins gently, and they made their way through the castle gates onto the property.

Here goes nothing, Kristyn thought.

As they made their way across the castle grounds, Kristyn noticed that everything was covered in a thick layer of ice. Tree branches bent under the weight of it. Blades of grass looked like sharp spikes sticking up from the ground. Animals and even people were frozen in their very tracks. Kristyn let out a low, shaky breath. These were not reassuring signs. It seemed that whoever came across the ice queen did not make it out to tell the tale.

"Now I know where everyone goes for the winter!" Hilarion joked, trying to lighten the mood.

Kristyn laughed nervously. But her mind was on Hailey. Where was the Queen keeping her? Would they be able to find her? Was she frozen, too?

Slowly, the trio approached a sparkling crystal door. Just then, the door creaked open, as if by magic. They peered inside and saw a long, dark hallway. *No telling where that leads,* Kristyn thought. But there was no turning back. Hailey needed her.

Kristyn hopped down from Albrecht's horse and turned to her companions. "Thank you for getting me here," she said sincerely. "The rest is up to me now."

"Don't go!" Hilarion cried, leaping off his horse and dropping to one knee in front of

Kristyn. "Think this over, please. We could be so happy together."

Kristyn shook her head. There just wasn't time for another round of marriage proposals!

Hilarion pressed on. He gestured toward Albrecht. "Either one of us could give you a happy life! With me," he continued, putting a hand across his chest, "you would be significantly more comfortable, but . . ."

Kristyn pulled Hilarion to his feet. He had a point—both of them would offer a very nice life to someone, someday. But she knew what she had to do. "I would never be happy if I didn't try to help my friend," she said softly. "That's what friends do."

Albrecht and Hilarion exchanged a look.

"Then we won't be happy unless we help you," Hilarion replied.

"Yes," Albrecht agreed. "We're all in this together."

Together, the three friends entered the icy palace.

Chapter 14

Kristyn's footsteps on the stone floor echoed as she made her way down a dark hallway and into the Snow Queen's throne room. She could see her breath in the frigid air. There were lines of frozen statues against each wall. Kristyn hoped she wouldn't end up like them.

"People don't call ahead anymore," the Snow Queen sneered from her throne in the center of the room. "They just show up from out of nowhere." She eyed Albrecht and Hilarion. "And you've brought friends."

Kristyn could hear Hilarion's teeth chattering behind the Queen. She wasn't sure if it was from the fear or the cold—probably both.

"And look at you," Albrecht replied, nervously gesturing at the statues. "With a houseful, and here we are, barging in." He gulped. "Where are our manners? Another time, perhaps?" he continued, backing out the doorway.

The Snow Queen shot an icy ray of magic toward Albrecht, stopping him in his tracks. She glared at Kristyn. "So, you're the one who's changing the stories, not following directions," she growled, eyes narrow. "Well, you're just in time for a show."

A show? Kristyn didn't like the sound of that.

The Snow Queen pulled a cord next to her throne. A curtain swung open behind her.

Kristyn gasped. Hailey stood frozen on a platform, her feet touching at their heels in perfect first position.

The Snow Queen grinned evilly. "What do you think, Giselle? Or is it Odette?"

Kristyn ran forward. "Let her go!" she yelled. "I'm the one you want!"

The Snow Queen rose from her throne and walked toward Hailey. "I've taught her the correct way to pirouette. She takes direction perfectly."

To demonstrate, the Snow Queen twirled her finger, setting the frozen Hailey in motion— she spun around in a precise pirouette.

"Perrrrfect," the Snow Queen purred. "Now do a hundred more."

On command, Hailey spun faster and faster.

"She's not a dancer!" Kristyn cried.

"Everyone has to start somewhere," the Snow Queen replied.

"That's not what she wants." Kristyn pictured Hailey back in Madame Katerina's costume shop, happily stitching together satin and tulle. Hailey didn't love the stage the way Kristyn did. Her passion was behind the scenes. And now Kristyn's longing for the spotlight might have cost Hailey her dream. What had she done? Kristyn felt a lump rise in her throat.

"But it's what I want," the Snow Queen replied icily. Working Hailey like a puppet, she spun her faster and faster.

"Stop!" Kristyn shouted, rushing toward the Queen.

The Snow Queen dropped her finger, and

Hailey instantly collapsed in a heap. Kristyn raced to her side and knelt down.

But the Snow Queen wasn't done yet. She raised her finger once more, this time aiming it directly at Kristyn. "Now it's your turn," she cackled.

The Snow Queen swirled her finger, and Kristyn rose at her command. Music swelled. As the Snow Queen wished, Kristyn performed pas de chats, arabesques, and pliés. And then came the pirouettes. She turned faster and faster until she thought her legs would crumble underneath her.

"Not bad," the Snow Queen murmured all the while. "Perrrrfect."

Hilarion dashed toward the Queen. "Let her go!" he ordered.

The Snow Queen spun on her heel to face him. She shot him with an icy blast, hurling him across the room.

"See?" the Queen said, returning her attention to Kristyn. "You can do it."

Kristyn eyed the Queen. Her body might

have been caught in the Queen's spell, but her mind was still very much her own.

As the Queen raised her fingers again, Kristyn closed her eyes. She pictured all that was dear to her heart about dance: the stage, the warm lights overhead, the way the music made her feel like she was floating above the world. As she felt the familiar surge of joy take over, she changed directions, breaking the Snow Queen's spell.

"What?" the Snow Queen screeched, redoubling her efforts. "How did you do that?"

Kristyn smiled as she let the natural rhythm of dance envelope her. She glided across the platform in her signature expressive style. The music pulsed through her.

"Stop that!" the Snow Queen commanded. "There is only one way."

That's what you think, Kristyn thought as she performed a grand jette in the opposite direction. She began to pirouette once more, faster and faster. Suddenly, she was engulfed in swirls of magic—but not the Snow Queen's kind. As she twirled, her outfit changed into a flowing pink costume, matching her shoes perfectly.

"No!" the Snow Queen cried hysterically. "There is only one way this tale can end! With your power to change stories and my power to freeze time, we can rule everything!"

So that was what she was after! But Kristyn wasn't interested in ruling the world. All she wanted was to dance the only way she'd ever known how—her way.

A dense, warm fog began to fill the Snow Queen's throne room. It wrapped itself around the Queen, causing her to fade away.

Kristyn slowed down and stopped in a graceful arabesque. "My name is Kristyn," she declared evenly as the Snow Queen disappeared. "And I write my own story."

Chapter 15

As the fog cleared, Kristyn ran to Hailey's side.
"What happened?" Hailey asked groggily.

Kristyn handed Hailey her sewing glasses. "Everything's okay now," Kristyn reassured her friend. And the more she looked around, the more she actually believed it.

The frozen statues in the room began to thaw as villagers were brought back to life. They were no longer victims of the Snow Queen's power.

Hilarion stepped toward Kristyn. "Thank you for what you did," he said.

"Yes, we all thank you," one of the villagers echoed.

Kristyn smiled warmly. "Thank you all for helping me," she replied.

"Is there any more dancing you'd like to do?"

Hailey teased Kristyn, a glint in her eyes.

Kristyn giggled. "Yes, but not here." She knew what she needed to do. She bent down to untie her pink toe shoes. "Let's go home," she said, just as the magic made everything blurry.

Soon, Kristyn and Hailey were standing in Madame Katerina's warm, dusty costume shop. They looked around. Everything was just as they'd left it.

Hailey rubbed her eyes. "Did we just . . . ?" she asked, trying to make sense of all they had been through.

Kristyn laughed. "Yes, I think we did."

They stared at Kristyn's pink shoes suspiciously.

Just then, Tara came breezing into the shop. "There you are!" she cried. "I've been looking all over for you." She shoved a pair of pale pink toe shoes into Kristyn's hands. "You're a size five, right? I brought these for you. They're from last season—I wasn't going to use them." She paused and looked down at Kristyn's feet. "Oh, you've already got some."

Kristyn smiled. "No—these look great," she replied, clutching Tara's shoes in her hands. "Thanks—that was really nice."

Tara shrugged. "Break a leg," she said, spinning on her heel and almost crashing into Madame Katerina. The costume designer was covered head to toe in tutus, as usual. She smiled at the girls.

"Madame Katerina," Kristyn started. She wasn't sure where to begin. "The shoes . . . Tara . . . Odile. Did I . . . did we . . . ?"

Madame Katerina waved her hand, cutting off Kristyn. "I don't know what you are talking about. But I do know, Kristyn, that it's your turn for the showcase in fifteen minutes. Hailey, please help her into her costume."

Hailey nodded. "Right. But first I have to make a few alterations," she said.

Kristyn looked hopefully at Madame Katerina.

"Good. Follow your instincts," Madame

Katerina replied, smiling warmly at the girls.

Hailey and Kristyn grinned and disappeared down a costume aisle.

A few moments later, Kristyn stood in the wings of the stage, trying to keep her jitters at bay. She could see the international ballet scouts sitting in the front row of the audience. Her chance to dance in the showcase was coming up, and she hoped to impress them.

Taking a deep, calming breath, Kristyn focused on Tara and Dillon, who were halfway through their *Swan Lake* pas de deux. Kristyn watched as Tara gracefully glided in front of Dillon, and he lifted her effortlessly into the air.

"That's it . . . that's it," Kristyn whispered as Dillon gently placed Tara back on the ground.

She felt genuinely happy for Tara and Dillon. All of their practice was paying off; their dancing was flawless.

In the audience, Kristyn could see the scouts

nodding in approval. Behind them, she saw Tara's father nervously munching on his turkey jerky.

Suddenly, Hailey popped up behind Kristyn, causing her to jump.

"I've got your dress," Hailey whispered in her ear. "Quick! Come on." She tugged Kristyn by the arm and the two disappeared backstage.

Kristyn entered the costume-change booth backstage. She closed the curtain just as she heard the audience erupt in applause. *Tara and Dillon must be finished,* she thought. Judging from the clapping and cheering, she guessed they had nailed it. She smiled to herself and reached for her costume on the hook. She touched the lace of her new dress and marveled at Hailey's careful stitching. It was stunning. *If my dancing is even half as beautiful as this costume, I'll be happy,* she thought, slipping it over her head. She turned to look in the mirror, smoothing the satin apron, and grinned. *Time to shine.*

She pulled open the curtain and stepped out of the changing booth, almost smacking right into Tara and Dillon as they rushed backstage.

"Wow!" Tara cried, impressed by Kristyn's costume. "Get out there, and make magic."

Dillon grinned and gave Kristyn a hug. "You're going to knock 'em dead," he said.

Just then, the stage manager appeared and pointed at Kristyn. "Milkmaid finale! Places!" she announced.

Kristyn smiled nervously at Hailey. This was their big moment. Everything they'd been working for rested on this one dance. Hailey added one more bobby pin to Kristyn's bun, and then clasped her hands. "Feel the music and flow," she said. "Remember—have fun!"

Kristyn nodded and hurried onto the stage.

Chapter 16

Kristyn took her place under the lights next to her cow prop. She crossed her arms against her chest, pointed her toe to the side, and took a deep breath.

The curtain rose, and she heard the familiar hush of the audience. *I was born to do this,* she thought, feeling suddenly calm. The music swelled and she began to spin. As the melody whirled around her, she picked up speed and glided through her routine with the grace of a swan. Out of the corner of her eye, she saw Madame Natasha nodding and the ballet scouts checking their programs, looking for her name. She beamed as all her joy, passion, and strength flowed in time to the music.

Suddenly, a cloud of glittering magic swirled

around Kristyn. She pirouetted, turning faster and faster as the magic churned. Her hair loosened and tumbled over her shoulders as her dress transformed into a bright pink tutu. A pink crown sparkled on her head, and bright pink shoes appeared on her feet. She heard the audience gasp in surprise and wonder.

At one with the music, Kristyn swept across the stage, arms spread wide. The music softened for a beat, and she took a deep breath, readying herself for her final move. As the music rose toward its close, Kristyn leaped through the air. She landed dramatically just as the music ended. *Perfect.*

Kristyn heard a stunned silence from the audience. She ventured a glance at Hailey in the wings. Had it looked as good as it had felt?

Hailey raised her arms and did a victory dance. *You did it!* she mouthed to Kristyn just as the audience erupted. They stood and applauded, giving Kristyn a standing ovation.

Kristyn's heart soared. She walked to the front of the stage and curtsied deeply as the audience threw roses at her feet.

Now, that's what I'm talking about!" Dillon shouted as he rushed onstage. He scooped Kristyn up in a giant hug and spun her around.

Kristyn laughed as he placed her back on her feet. Then she raced into the wings, grabbed Hailey's hand, and dragged her onstage. She pointed to her costume and back at Hailey, to show the audience who had made her look so beautiful.

Dillon escorted both ladies to the lip of the stage and swept his arm toward them, inviting the audience to applaud them both.

Kristyn curtsied gracefully once more as Hailey just blushed and giggled.

It was a night to remember.

Moments later, in the dressing area backstage, the other dancers crowded around Kristyn and Hailey.

"Nicely done, Kristyn," Tara said genuinely.

Kristyn smiled. "You too."

Just then, Kristyn heard the sound of Madame Natasha's heels clacking toward her. *Uh-oh.* She looked over her shoulder to see her instructor and the international ballet scouts approaching. Mr. Pennington was trailing behind them, talking a mile a minute.

". . . then when she was twelve, we actually moved to France for a year so Tara could dance," he was boasting.

Madame Natasha breezed into the center of the dressing area, carrying a bouquet of ruby-red roses in her arms.

"Ladies and gentlemen!" she announced, her French accent thick with the excitement of the evening. "The ballet company offers the roles of Giselle and Albrecht to Tara Pennington and Dillon Matthews!" She gave the roses to Tara and shook Dillon's hand. She opened her mouth to speak again, but one of the ballet scouts interrupted her.

"What's even more surprising," he began, working his way through the crowd, "is this new dance voice you've been hiding. Where's Kristyn?"

Hailey gave Kristyn a shove, and she stumbled to the front of the crowd.

The ballet scout took her hand. "I've been searching for something new," he continued. "And I didn't know what it was. And now I know it was you!"

Madame Natasha edged her way through the crowd, looking uneasy. "What you saw tonight was totally—"

"Totally unexpected!" exclaimed another scout. "Inspired. The best dancing I've seen in years. She took everything that came before it and gave it back to us—fresh."

Madame Natasha sighed, resigned. "That's Kristyn," she replied. "Always giving us something new."

The first ballet scout turned once again toward Kristyn. "I've been planning a new ballet, and I want to build it around you and your ideas. What do you think?"

Hailey hugged Dillon around the neck and

squealed. Tara dropped her bouquet in shock.

Kristyn was speechless. She never expected that dancing from the heart would lead to the part of a lifetime. "I would be honored," she finally replied.

The ballet scout nodded. "And we're going to need this dress," he added, pointing to Kristyn's costume.

Kristyn pulled Hailey into a hug. "We won't forget the dress!" she said, laughing.

The ballet scout shook Madame Natasha's hand. "Well done. Keep the talent coming," he said, making his way to the side exit. The other scouts followed behind him, leaving Madame Natasha alone with her dancers.

"Miss Faraday," Madame Natasha began. "I owe you an apology."

Kristyn shook her head. She and Madame hadn't always seen eye to eye, but Kristyn admired her instructor. "No, of course you don't."

"Yes, I do. I see now that I was trying to turn you into another Tara, but what I really needed was my first Kristyn." She held Kristyn's gaze for a moment then pulled her shawl tightly around her shoulders. "Class tomorrow starts promptly at nine-thirty! And bring your good ideas!" she announced, before spinning on her heel and disappearing.

Kristyn turned to Dillon. "Congrats on the Albrecht role," she said, laughing as Dillon pulled her into a bear hug.

"I always thought of myself as more of a Hilarion. Albrecht is kind of a jerk," Dillon admitted.

Kristyn smiled knowingly. "It turns out he's really nice. And he and Hilarion wind up being good friends in the end. Am I right, Hailey?"

Hailey nodded, grinning. "Who's hungry?" she asked.

Dillon raised his hand. "Ice cream in an hour?"

"I'm there," Kristyn answered, bending to untie her toe shoes.

Dillon and the rest of the dancers burst out of the stage door onto the street, leaving Kristyn and Hailey behind.

As the girls packed up, Madame Katerina appeared, pushing a rack of swan costumes back toward the costume shop.

"You need some help, Madame?" Hailey asked.

"Not at all," she replied. "You girls go ahead. I'm just tidying up. Thinking about giving these swans pink shoes for the next show," she said with a wink.

"Perrrrfect!" Kristyn agreed. She swung her dance bag across her shoulder and linked arms with Hailey. She took one last look across the stage and sighed. She could never have guessed how tonight would turn out. In fact, she wouldn't have believed it if she hadn't lived it all herself! But she knew one thing for sure: she had followed her heart. And with friends like Hailey standing beside her, *anything* was possible.

Epilogue

Madame Katerina entered her costume shop and made her way down the last aisle. She opened a door and pushed aside a rack of tutus to reveal a secret door. She turned a dial, entering the combination, and the entry swiveled open.

Madame Katerina ducked into the secret room. It was lined with row after row of antique shoe boxes. She replaced Kristyn's hot-pink toe shoes in an opening on the shelf and wiped her hands on her apron. Satisfied, she smiled and switched off the light. Another *magical* performance.

Ballet Glossary

arabesque: a position in which a dancer stands on one leg with the other leg extended behind the body with the knees straight

ballet company: a group of ballet dancers who perform together

barre: a horizontal bar at waist level on which ballet dancers rest a hand for support during exercises

choreography: the sequence of steps and movements in a dance

en pointe: on the tips of the toes

grande jette: a long horizontal jump

pas de chat: a leap in which the knees are bent out to the side and the toes are nearly touching

pas de deux: a dance for two people

pas de trois: a dance for three people

pirouette: a turn of the body while standing on one leg

plié: a bending of the knees with hips, legs, and feet turned outward

port de bras: the positions and movements of the arms

prima ballerina: the chief female dancer in a ballet or ballet company

toe shoes: ballet shoes that are specially designed with a flat tip to allow a dancer to stand on her toes

tutu: a ballet dancer's skirt, often worn with an attached bodice

I dance to my own beat

Ballet keeps me on my toes

at heart

believe in dance

dancer at heart

in the spotlight

dan

center stage her

believe in dance

shining star

twirl like a Barbie girl

Tu Tu Cute

dan

dancer at heart

believe in dance

dream it. dance it.

star

Love

believe in dance

ballet is the best

shining star

love to dance...

love to dream...

Love to

of a dancer

In the Spotlight

believe

center stage here I come

dance

Ballet keeps

Barbie

here I come

I dance

center

in the spotlight

to my own beat

Love to Dance

pointe your toes

ve to dance...

dancer at

I dance to my own beat

Ballet keeps me on my toes

believe in dance

at heart

shining star

dancer at heart

in the spotlight

dan

center stage her

believe in dance

shining star

twirl like a Barbie girl

Tu Tu Cute

dan

your toes

dancer at heart

believe in dance

dream it. dance it.

star

Love

believe in dance

ballet is the best

shining star

dancer at heart

Ballet keeps me on my toes

believe in dance

shining star

dancer at heart

in the spotlight

here I come

center

in the spotlight

believe in dance

Believe

shining star

dance and twirl like a Barbie girl

Tu Tu

pointe your toes

dancer at heart

believe

shining star

dream it. dance it.

Love

Barbie

believe in dance

shining star

ballet is the best

to Dance

love to dance... love to dream.

lieve in dance

of a dancer

In the Spotlight

dancer at heart

center stage here I come

keeps me on my toes

shining star

I dance

ter stage here I come

to my own beat

in the spotlight

pointe your toes

Love to Dance

love to dance...

dancer at

Barbie

I dance to my own be

Ballet keeps me on my toe

believe in dance

shining star

dancer at heart

in the spotli

ancer at heart

believe in dance

here I come

cente

in the spotlight

shining star

Believe

dance and twirl like a Barbie girl

Tu Tu

pointe your toes

dancer at heart

believe

dream it. dance it.

shining star

Love

Barbie

believe in dance

ballet is the best

shining star